In My Backyard

In My Backyard

John DeVries

Werner Zimmermann

SCHOLASTIC INC.
New York Toronto London Auckland Sydney

 Published by Scholastic Inc., 555 Broadway,
New York, NY 10012, by arrangement with Scholastic Canada Ltd.
Printed in the U.S.A.
ISBN 0-590-27867-3

20 19 14 01

To Wanita
John

To Mupps, all heart and understanding.
And to Klaus, without whose frog this book
could not have been.
Werner

In my backyard I have a frog.

My mother found him on a log.

I called my frog my good friend Jim.

My mummy yelled, “Get rid of him!”

I asked my dad if Jim could stay.

My daddy said, "Take him away!"

I asked my grandpa if I could keep . . .

Oh, he's asleep.

I showed my sister my good friend Jim.
She nearly ran right over him!

So!

I told my dog (his name is Rover)

that he would soon be moving over.

And now Jim lives
with my dog in his house

with his cat and my mouse

with his bowl and my pail

with his box and my nail

with his rope and my ring

with his ball and my string

with his rug and my coat

with his tub and my boat

with his rod and my reel

with his rake and my wheel

with his pole and my flag

with his hole in my bag.

Rover, you're a pal!